Arlene Phillips OBE is a world-renowned director and choreographer creating musicals, videos, films, television programming and spectaculars. Her inventive choreography has been seen in the musicals *Grease*, *We Will Rock You*, *Starlight Express*, *The Sound of Music*, *Flashdance* and *The Wizard of Oz*. Her screen work includes the films *Annie* and *Legend*, and the television shows *DanceX* and *Britannia High*. Arlene's videos have starred everyone from Robbie Williams to Elton John, Whitney Houston to Tina Turner. Her largest ever spectacular was the XVII Commonwealth Games. She is known throughout the UK as a former judge on *Strictly Come Dancing* and now on *So You Think You Can Dance?* Her favourite job, however, has been as mother to her two daughters, Alana and Abi.

First published in 2011
by Faber and Faber Limited
Bloomsbury House
74–77 Great Russell Street
London WC1B 3DA

Typeset by Baobab Editorial and Design
Printed in England by Bookmarque, Croydon, UK

Text and illustrations © Arlene Phillips, 2011
Illustrations by Pixie Potts

With thanks to Susan Reuben

The right of Arlene Phillips to be identified as author of this work
has been asserted in accordance with Section 77 of the Copyright,
Designs and Patents Act 1988

A CIP record for this book
is available from the British Library

978–0–571–226081–2

2 4 6 8 10 9 7 5 3 1

Twilight Tango

By Arlene Phillips

Illustrated by Pixie Potts

faber and faber

Miss Trina

Keisha

Matthew

Verity

The Students at Step Out Studio

Alana

Meena

Chloe

Toby

For

Tyler Appleby,
Adam Arbouhat,
Amilcar Brown,
Myesha Chowdhury,
Jordan Clarke,
Mewael Eyob,
Dannie Hagan,
Kaitlin Harvey,
Gloria Kitaka,
Lily McIntyre,
Jordan McMahon,
Shannia Salcedo-Valencia,
Jorge Salvatore,
and Danny Swan,

from Blessed Sacrament Primary School, London.

Chapter 1

'Hurry up, Mum, pleeease!' Alana begged from the back of the car.

'Alana!' snapped Mum. 'There is a thirty-mile-an-hour speed limit, and I'm not going to go any faster.'

'But I'll be late for dance class! Miss Trina will be so cross!'

'You won't get to dance class at all if I crash the car and put us both in hospital!'

Alana was desperate to get to Step Out

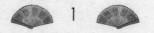

Studio that evening. Last week they'd
started learning the tango and Alana had
loved every minute of it. She'd spent the
whole week looking forward to learning
some more steps.

'I'm finishing work early this evening,
so I can drive you to your dance lesson,'
Mum had said that morning.

But then the bell had rung for the end
of school and there was no sign of her.
She hadn't appeared until fifteen minutes
later, by which time Alana was totally
frustrated.

'Sorry, darling,' she'd said. 'My boss
made me stay late and I didn't like to
complain. I can't afford to lose this job.'

Alana sighed. Why couldn't she have
a normal mother who baked cupcakes,

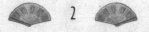

helped with her homework and did things when she said she would?

Mum turned on the radio. It was the local drivetime show.

'Roll up, all you talented kids!' the DJ was saying. 'The Town Gala is taking place in six weeks' time. We need singers, actors, dancers, gymnasts . . . you name it. So if you love to perform, then limber up, learn your lines and put your leotards on. Your town needs YOU!'

Alana was only half listening. She kept looking at her watch and imagining Miss Trina starting the class without her. As soon as Mum parked outside the door of Step Out Studio, she leapt out. 'Thanks, Mum!' she yelled, and dashed inside.

But when she entered the rehearsal

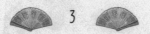

3

room, she stopped short. It was obvious straight away that something was wrong. Instead of doing their warm-up exercises or practising their tango, the students were standing in little huddles, muttering to each other. They didn't even notice her come in.

Miss Trina was sitting glumly on a chair at the front. Her hair, which was usually shiny and tightly tied back, hung limply round her face and she wasn't wearing any make-up. Worst of all was her expression. She looked . . . *helpless*,

was the only way to describe it. And Miss Trina *never* looked helpless – she always appeared to be completely in control.

Alana rushed over to her best friend Meena, who was whispering to Keisha. 'What is it?' she hissed. 'What's happened?'

Meena turned towards her and gripped her wrist. 'It's Step Out Studio,' she replied, her eyes wide. 'It might have to close!'

'WHAT? Close? No! Why?' stuttered Alana.

'It's awful,' replied Meena. 'Miss Trina told us that the Studio has been struggling for a while to keep going because there just aren't enough students. But now the people who own the building have put their rent up, and that's made things a lot worse. Unless she can recruit some more pupils, she's not going to be able to pay them – and there isn't anywhere else in the town suitable for a dance school.'

'But that's terrible!' moaned Alana. 'What can we do? We have to think of something!'

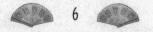

'Miss Trina has asked us to come up with some ideas,' Meena replied. 'But I simply can't imagine what we're going to be able to do about it, other than tell our friends in case they want to join.'

Just then, Toby raised his hand and everyone fell silent.

'What is it, Toby?' asked Miss Trina.

'Perhaps we could put an advert on the telly to get some more kids to join,' suggested Toby.

'Where do you think Miss Trina's going to find the money to do that,' sneered Verity, 'if she can't even afford to run the studio?'

'I know!' piped up Chloe. 'Maybe we could all do a dance routine in the town centre – sort of like busking – and people

7

could throw us coins. Then we could use them to pay the studio rent! It would be fun!'

'If you think my father is going to let me dance in the street, begging for money, you must be crazy,' said Verity, scornfully.

'That's enough, Verity,' rapped out Miss Trina, regaining her usual tone of authority. Then she turned to Toby and Chloe. 'I don't think those ideas would really work,' she said gently. 'We're going to have to keep thinking.'

Alana wasn't listening to the suggestions. She was sitting cross-legged on the floor, staring into space, her brow furrowed in concentration. She felt completely wretched. For one thing,

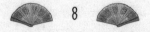

dancing was the most important thing
in the world to her and she didn't know
how she'd survive if Step Out Studio
no longer existed. And even worse, Miss
Trina had given Alana a free place
because she was such a talented dancer.
Her mum couldn't afford to send her
otherwise. Now Alana felt as though she
would be a burden to the dance school if
it was so short of money.

She *had* to think of a solution. As she pondered, the voice of the DJ she'd been listening to in the car drifted into her head. 'Roll up roll up . . . talented kids . . .'

Suddenly, she leapt in the air, making everyone jump. 'I've got it!' she cried.

'Well, make sure we don't get it too,' sniggered Verity.

Alana ignored the interruption. 'The Town Gala!' she announced, as though this explained everything.

Miss Trina raised her eyebrows, looking interested for the first time. 'What about the Town Gala?' she asked.

'Well, you know how there's going to be that big gala next month at the Open Air Theatre, and there'll be hundreds of kids performing?' Alana continued, her words falling over each other in her haste. 'There's going to be singing, acting, everything . . .'

'Yes, go on . . .' said Miss Trina encouragingly.

'Well, there'll be loads of parents coming to watch their children perform, so if the Step Out Studio dancers did a routine there, it would be a really good way to advertise the dance school. It's bound to attract more students to join.'

'I think you've found the answer, Alana!' exclaimed Miss Trina. She stood up and clapped her hands, briskly. 'Now, everybody,' she said. 'There's no time to waste. Into position please. We'll do a ballroom routine at the Gala; let's work on the tango. It's a dance bursting with

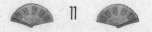

energy and drive and the perfect thing to persuade the parents and kids that Step Out Studio is an amazing place to be! We're going to have to work hard at it, though!'

Miss Trina got everyone to find their partners and get into tango hold. It was a difficult dance needing sharp head turns, flexed knees and a strong lead from the boys.

'Well, it didn't take Miss Trina long to start shouting out counts,' Toby muttered to Alana as they got dizzy practising their pivots. 'I was quite looking forward to a week where we didn't have to work hard.'

Alana could see, though, that Toby looked excited. He didn't normally enjoy dancing – he only went to Step Out

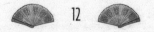

Studio because his mum made him – but he did like showing off, and what better way to show off than to perform the tango to a huge audience at the Open Air Theatre?

Chapter 2

Alana spent the week practising tango steps in her bedroom.

The day before the next class, she was in her room working on her heel swivels when her mum came in, looking worried. She sat on the bed, and patted the duvet for Alana to sit beside her.

'I've just had an email from Miss Trina,' she explained. 'She's had an accident – someone bumped into her on an escalator in the shopping centre and knocked her off balance. She fell all the way down.'

'Oh no!' cried Alana. 'Is she badly hurt?'

'Not seriously, but she has broken her leg. She has to stay in bed for at least the next two weeks, so there are going to be no Step Out Studio classes for the time being. There's no way she can afford to get a substitute teacher.'

'Poor Miss Trina,' Alana groaned. 'And what about the Gala? How are we going to be able to put a tango routine together without a teacher?'

'It looks like Step Out Studio is going to have to pull out,' replied Mum sympathetically.

'But we can't!' wailed Alana, close to tears. 'I have to call Meena.' And she

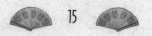

dashed to the phone.

'Don't chat for hours!' Mum called after her.

Alana sighed. Mum tried her best, but she could never understand how important dancing was to Alana.

When Meena came to the phone,

 16

Alana didn't take the time to say 'hello'. 'Have you heard the news?' she cried.

'Yes, Mum just came in and told me. It's awful! Poor Miss Trina! And what about the Gala?'

'I know!' groaned Alana. 'And the posters have already been printed with Step Out Studio on them. I know they have cos I saw one up in the library. So if we pull out now, it'll look completely rubbish – it might even put off new students who had been thinking of coming! We *have* to think of a way to perform at the Gala!'

'But how?' wailed Meena. 'We barely know how to do the tango. We've only been practising the dance for two weeks.'

'And the poster says *Tangotastic! by the*

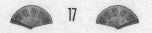

17

students of Step Out Studio,' added Alana. 'So we can hardly come on doing the waltz or something!'

The girls said nothing for a minute. They were both deep in thought as they tried to come up with a plan. There's only one thing for it, thought Alana. I'm going to have to see if Madame Coco can help.

'Meena, I've gotta go,' she announced.

'Why?' asked Meena. 'Have you had an idea?'

'Erm, not really,' Alana replied, vaguely. 'There's just someone I need to talk to.'

Alana put the phone down and pulled on her trainers. 'I've got to go out, Mum!' she shouted.

'But Alana,' called Mum. 'You're meant to be giving Abi her supper later, remember,

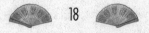

18

and helping with her homework!'

Alana often had to take care of her little sister so their mum could study. She loved Abi but it was a complete pain having to look after her so often.

'It's all right, Mum,' she replied. 'I won't be long!'

And she ran out of the door and along to the corner of her street, to Madame Coco's Costume Emporium.

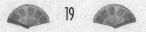

19

Chapter 3

Alana pushed open the shop door and
immediately she was hit by a wall of
noise. The shop was completely crammed
with little girls aged about six or seven,
wearing ballet costumes and chattering
like mad. A harassed-looking lady –
presumably their teacher – was flapping
her hands about, trying to keep them
in control, but not succeeding. And
Madame Coco was rushing here and

there, grabbing piles of leotards and pale pink satin ballet shoes of all sizes and handing them out to be tried on. She looked almost as stressed as the teacher. When she caught sight of Alana, however, her face broke into a broad smile and she pushed her way through to greet her.

'My favourite customer!' she exclaimed, kissing Alana on both cheeks.

'Hello, Madame Coco!' grinned Alana, feeling a bit embarrassed, because she wasn't really a customer at all. She had never bought anything from the Costume Emporium – Madame Coco always insisted on lending her the costumes she needed and she never had to pay.

'Now, can you wait for me a few minutes?' asked Madame Coco. 'I must

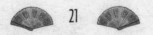

21

finish dealing with these children. They
are the pupils of Signora Campanella's
Ballet School. They are buying outfits for
their performance at the Town Gala.'

Alana sat down in the pink velvet
armchair and watched in amazement
as Madame Coco kitted out every
child with a brand-new outfit. Signora
Campanella's school clearly had plenty

of money. When the Step Out Studio students did a show, they had to make do with a mixture of the dance clothes they already had at home and anything they could find in the Studio costume and props cupboard.

As soon as the last child had been fitted with a costume, and their teacher had paid and shepherded them out of the door, Madame Coco breathed a sigh of relief. 'Now, ma chérie,' she said. 'Tell me your news.'

Alana took a deep breath and explained to her everything that had been going on. Step Out Studio's money problems and her idea to perform the tango – then Miss Trina's accident, which would probably mean they couldn't

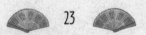

appear at the Gala after all.

Halfway through, Madame Coco made Alana pause. She disappeared into the back of the shop, then returned with a tall glass of passion-fruit juice, which she handed to Alana. 'Carry on,' she said listening intently.

When Alana had finished her story, Madame Coco sat there looking thoughtful. Then she sprang up and started grabbing things from the rails and shelves.

'Go and put these on, ma chérie,' she said, and before Alana knew what was happening, Madame Coco had piled a huge bundle of rose-pink netting in her arms, and balanced a pair of satin ballroom shoes and a pink-beaded choker on the top.

'But Madame
Coco,' replied
Alana, gloomily,
'there's no
point me
having a beautiful tango
costume when there's no one
to teach us the tango. I don't see
how it will help to save Step Out Studio.'

'Alana,' said Madame Coco, bending
down so she could look her straight in the
eye. 'Do you trust me?'

'Well, of course, Madame Coco, more
than anyone,' replied Alana.

'So go and put on the costume, just
for me.'

Alana sighed, but she did as she was told.

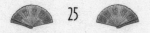

In the changing room she shook out
the dress, and smiled in spite of herself. It
was like something Cinderella might have
worn to the ball. The top half was covered
in pink sequins, and the skirt was made
of layers and layers of frothy netting
that reached almost to the ground. Alana
fastened the choker round her neck and
slipped on the shoes. Then she returned to
the shop floor, feeling a bit self-conscious.

'Very pretty.' Madame Coco nodded,
looking at her approvingly. 'We will fasten
your hair like so,' she said, and she swept
it into a low bun, and secured it with a
huge pink and white flower.

'Now, ma petite,' she said when she was
finished. 'Imagine you are in Argentina
and show me some tango steps. I want

you to pretend that you've been dancing the tango your whole life.'

'That could be tricky, seeing as I hadn't danced a step of it until two weeks ago!' Alana replied. But she closed her eyes anyway and stood in the tango hold, imagining her partner opposite her. Then hesitantly she began to dance the steps that Miss Trina had taught them.

And as she danced, her movements became quicker and more confident. All at once, the floor seemed to melt away from beneath her feet. She felt a tingling sensation through her whole body, and she could hear Madame Coco's voice calling, 'Remember, ma petite, when your good deed is done, the call of home will beckon. You will return home! You will return home!'

The words grew fainter and fainter, but
still she danced. Then suddenly her feet
hit the floor again, and a wave of warm,
muggy air swept over her. She opened
her eyes and gave a squeal of alarm.
Madame Coco's shop had vanished, and
instead she was in a dusty street, crowded
with people.

Chapter 4

Everyone stopped moving and stared in
amazement at the girl with the exotic
costume who seemed to have appeared
from nowhere. Before Alana had time to
think, she felt a tugging at her dress and
an awful ripping noise. A small scruffy
dog had torn a great piece of netting
from her skirt and had scampered off with
it, wagging its tail furiously.

'Oy!' yelled Alana, and dashed after

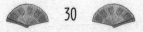

it. What would Madame Coco say? she thought frantically. She couldn't return with a torn dress. After a long chase the dog disappeared inside a small building. She dashed in after it, then skidded to a halt. She was in a small, stuffy room, and a group of people were looking at her in astonishment.

'Your dog tore a piece off my dress,' she explained. Or at least, that is what she meant to say, but the words came out in another language.

A tall, good-looking boy a little older than her stepped forward. 'Drop it!' he commanded the dog. The dog dropped the piece of pink netting – now looking extremely soggy – on the floor and the boy picked it up. 'Mama, do you think it is possible to sew this back on?' he asked.

'But of course!' replied a plump lady. 'And in the meantime, my dear,' she added, turning to Alana, 'you must sit down and rest.'

She offered her a drink in a hollowed-out shell. Alana sucked it tentatively through a straw and found that the warm

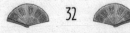

liquid tasted a bit like tea and was very soothing. 'It's called *maté*,' the mother told her. 'You can have some more after we share it round.'

The maté was passed from person to person to take a sip, but no one took their eyes off Alana. Alana counted eight family members – the mother and seven children. The younger ones stared at her as if she had jumped straight out of a fairytale.

Alana's mind raced. Where was she? There was no doubt she was in a hot country – the steamy atmosphere made that clear. The home she was in seemed to consist of a single room. There was one large bed, some rickety shelves and a small electric hob in the corner, but

no table to sit at. The paint was flaking
from the walls and it was obvious that the
family were very poor.

Alana decided to tell them that she was
lost, so it wouldn't look too odd to ask
where she was.

'We are just outside Buenos Aires,'
explained the boy.

Alana dragged her mind back to her

geography lessons. Buenos Aires – that's
in Argentina. And so we must be speaking
Spanish, she thought.

'Perhaps if you are not in too much
of a hurry, I could show you around,'
suggested the boy shyly.

'I'd love that!' exclaimed Alana.

'I am Miguel, by the way,' he said.

'Alana,' replied Alana, and they shook

hands and smiled.

As they headed outside, Miguel
told Alana that he was fourteen. He had
already left school, and was trying to
help support his family finding odd jobs
wherever he could, while his father was
away looking for work. But what he
loved more than anything was to dance
the tango.

'And you are a tango dancer too, I see,'
he added, nodding at her costume.

'Erm, no not really,' began Alana. 'The
thing is . . .'

'And no doubt,' interrupted Miguel, 'you are here to take part in the Junior Latin Dance Championships.'

'Er, actually I'm not,' Alana replied.

'But that is wonderful!' exclaimed Miguel. 'I wish more than anything to take part in the championships, but I have no partner. The people round here are poor and there is no one who can pay for the coaching.' He turned to Alana. 'Will you be my partner?' he begged.

'But that's what I was trying to tell you,' replied Alana a little desperately. 'I'm not a tango dancer. I've only ever had two tango lessons. I've had lots of training, but not in this particular dance.'

'But if you are a trained dancer, then you will be quick to learn the tango!'

Miguel insisted. 'I will teach you! Let us try, at least?'

Alana didn't think it would be possible, but how could she say no?

'OK, we can try,' she replied, doubtfully.

Miguel looked thrilled. 'There is a clearing a little way away,' he said. 'That is where we will have our lesson. We must begin at once.'

As they walked along the dusty path, Alana looked around her. There were rows and rows of makeshift homes – very small, but brightly painted. They were all built close together, with washing lines strung between them. Children ran barefoot along the dusty street, and stopped to stare at Alana in her sparkly costume. The more they stared, the more self-conscious she became.

While they walked, Miguel started to tell Alana about himself.

'My family have always loved to dance,' he explained. 'In fact, my grandfather was a famous tango dancer – famous all over the world. He was the one who taught me how to dance.' Miguel had a faraway look in his eyes and Alana could tell that he was thinking about something sad.

'What happened to him?' she asked, gently.

'His ship sank,' Miguel replied quietly. 'He was on his way to Europe, where he'd been invited to perform in Paris. He never trusted aeroplanes, so he always travelled by sea. The ship hit a rock, and down it went – taking him and his fortune with it. So my family were forced to leave our comfortable home.'

'Oh . . . I'm sorry,' Alana replied.

'It's OK,' continued Miguel, trying to smile. 'I miss him – we all do – but I have continued to practise the tango, in honour of his memory. And performing in this competition would mean everything to me. I know he would have wanted me to.'

Alana was feeling more and more nervous. So much was riding on the championships and she really hoped she wouldn't let Miguel down.

By the time they arrived at the clearing, the light was beginning to fade. The air was still extremely warm and muggy. A group of little boys were kicking a football to each other, but when

they saw Miguel and Alana, they stopped to watch what they were doing.

'Now,' said Miguel, 'what you must always remember is that the tango is a dance full of spirit and drama. However well you perform the steps, if you do not put all your emotions into the dance, it will have no meaning.'

As they moved together around the clearing, Alana concentrated hard to follow Miguel's steps.

'There must be no rise and fall,' Miguel warned as they danced. 'Just sharp

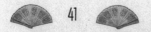

staccato movements with lots of changes of direction.'

They went over and over the steps, and Alana started to get a feel for the excitement of the dance. 'That's good!' said Miguel, approvingly.

The sun slipped below the horizon and people wandered out of their homes to watch the dancing couple. Someone

brought out a guitar and strummed a tango melody. A few other couples started to dance as well. A man appeared with an accordion and as the air filled with music, Alana began to understand the true spirit of the tango. In the twilight, the houses no longer looked so shabby and Alana felt almost as though she were in a scene from a film.

Only when the light had completely faded did Miguel come to a standstill. 'We must sleep,' he said, 'or we will not have enough energy for the competition tomorrow.'

He led Alana back to his home where his mum had made a steaming pot of bean stew. As Alana sat on the floor with the others to eat, she tried to separate out the members of the family. There was a girl older than Miguel who seemed nearly grown-up – then twin girls of about ten who couldn't stop staring at Alana's dress, a boy who looked about Abi's age, a toddler and a baby. Everyone talked at once without seeming particularly concerned about whether the others were listening. Most of the chat was about Miguel and Alana and the championships. The whole family was incredibly excited that Miguel was going to take part. Miguel's mum said that she would mend Alana's dress and get Miguel's grandfather's competition costume ready for Miguel to wear the next day.

'And we will all come to watch you,' she added.

'But how can we afford this?' asked Miguel.

'I have a little money saved,' she replied. 'Something tells me that this is the occasion to spend it. Your grandfather would have wanted us all to be there.'

After supper, the children helped clear things away. It was clear that each of them had a specific job to do. Without being asked, three of them washed up at an outside tap and two more spread blankets on the floor for sleeping. Miguel's big sister changed the baby's nappy before giving him to her mother to feed.

When she was ready to sleep, Miguel lent Alana a T-shirt and shorts and she

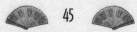

draped her tango costume carefully over a chair. Thank goodness no time passes at home while I'm having one of Madame Coco's adventures, she thought to herself as she lay down. Otherwise Mum would be worried sick.

Alana stared at the ceiling, which was made of sheets of corrugated iron with bits of sky peeping through the cracks. On one side of her was Miguel's older sister, and on the other side one of the twins. In the double bed were Miguel's mother, the toddler and the baby. It's amazing, thought Alana, that Miguel's family are being so kind to me. They have so little but they don't mind sharing what they have.

Chapter 5

The next thing Alana knew, the sun was filtering through the gaps in the ceiling and there was a huge bustle going on around her.

'Ah, you are awake,' exclaimed Miguel's mother when she saw her eyes were open. 'Come and have some breakfast. This is a special day. You and Miguel will need plenty of strength.'

Alana saw that Miguel was already

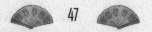

dressed in his grandfather's costume. His mother had, he explained, spent half the night altering it so it would fit him. He looked proud, if a bit self-conscious, in a polo-neck leotard, a beautifully cut pair of trousers and a double-breasted jacket with a crimson silk handkerchief in the breast pocket.

Miguel's sister handed Alana a cup of milky coffee, and some hot toast covered with a spread that looked like runny toffee. '*Dulce de leche* it's called,' she said. Alana took a bite of the

 48

toast. It was delicious.

As soon as breakfast was finished, Alana changed into Madame Coco's tango costume. Miguel's mum had mended it so expertly that you could barely see where it had been torn. Then the entire family set out to the place where the championships were being held.

They piled on to a bus heading for the centre of Buenos Aires. Someone got up to give Miguel's mother a seat with her baby, and everyone else stood in the aisle and held on tight. People smiled when they saw Miguel and Alana in their costumes. The whole city knew about the championships that day, so it was obvious where the family was going.

Miguel and Alana stood together,

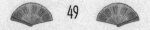

holding tight to straps above their heads as the bus swayed round corners. 'The theatre where the competition is being held is called the Coliseo,' Miguel told her. 'It is a popular theatre in our city'.

When they reached their stop, they piled off the bus. 'Buena suerte!' called one or two of the other passengers. 'Good luck!' Miguel and Alana nodded and smiled.

But when Alana turned round and saw the theatre, she stopped smiling. It towered above her, with tall colonnades, ornate windows and domed roofs. It looked incredibly impressive and intimidating. Could she really perform a dance she barely knew in this grand place? 'I have to,' she said to herself. 'For Miguel's sake.'

Taking a deep breath, she followed the

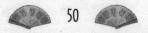

family through the grand doors.

Inside, behind a desk, a row of officials were recording details of the contestants. Alana didn't know what to reply when she was asked to give her address, so she just said it was the same as Miguel's.

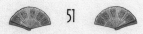

'You will be the third couple to dance in your category,' the official told them. And he gave them both a little number '3' to pin to their costume. Then they were pointed towards a rehearsal room where they could practise.

Miguel's mum hugged them both goodbye, then she led the rest of the family off to wait for the competition to start.

Miguel and Alana made their way to the rehearsal room. Inside, scores of children were doing exercises and practising their routines. Everyone who wasn't dancing was chatting excitedly.

A tall girl with an elaborate green dress looked Miguel and Alana up and down. 'What's THAT?' she asked with a smirk, staring at Miguel's costume.

'It is my costume, of course,' replied Miguel.

'It looks like something out of the last century,' sniggered the girl.

Miguel flushed and looked angry. 'This costume belonged to my grandfather!' he declared.

'I can tell!' laughed the girl, and flounced off, tossing her hair.

Miguel stood there staring after her, his fists clenched.

'Never mind her,' whispered Alana, putting her hand on his arm. 'We need to warm up.'

As they did some leg stretches, one of the other boys starting chatting. 'Where is your coach?' he asked.

'We don't have one,' Miguel replied.

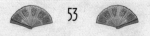

'You don't have one?' interrupted his partner who had overheard. 'You think you stand a chance in this competition when you don't even have a proper coach? We have been training with ours three times a week for the last year!'

Before Miguel had a chance to reply, Alana took him by the elbow. 'Come with me!' she hissed. She led him out of the

rehearsal room and along a corridor, where they found some stairs leading into the basement.

'Where are

we going?' demanded Miguel.

'To find somewhere to practise away from all those rich idiots!' Alana replied.

Miguel smiled, for the first time since they'd arrived.

In the basement, they found a deserted room that was obviously used for storage, and there the two of them went through their tango routine, in among dusty rails of costumes and old props.

'That's right, Alana,' said Miguel as they danced. 'We must move absolutely as one on the promenade. Remember your heel leads. Don't forget to keep your knees flexed and I want to see sharp head turns.'

Alana concentrated as hard as she could. They practised the routine over and over until at last it was time to go and

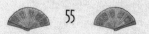

wait in the wings for their turn.

'This is it!' declared Miguel, smiling nervously.

'I hope I'm going to be good enough,' sighed Alana.

'Whatever happens,' Miguel replied, looking her straight in the eye, 'I will never forget that you were willing to do this for me. I will always remember it.'

Miguel and Alana were entered into the 'Under 16s' section of the championships, so there were many dancers a few years older than Alana. The other couples waiting in the wings looked incredibly grown-up and confident. They made Alana feel even more nervous than she was already.

They watched the first two couples

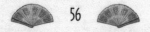

dance. Alana could see that they had been very thoroughly trained. Their moves were slick and well rehearsed.

She glanced across at Miguel. He wasn't watching what was going on on stage. His eyes were closed and his lips were moving. He looked like he might be praying. Then he made the sign of the cross, opened his eyes and smiled encouragingly at Alana.

All too soon it was their turn. Alana walked to the middle of the stage with Miguel and they stood in the tango hold, waiting for the music to begin. She looked out into the auditorium and her knees went wobbly. It was enormous, with row after row of red plush seats. There were two tiers of curved balconies, and the

ceiling was intricately painted and hung with chandeliers. Most terrifyingly of all, every seat was occupied. There must be 2,000 people watching us, thought Alana.

The front row of seats had been removed, and in their place was a table for the judges. There were five – three women and two men – each one staring unsmilingly at Alana and Miguel as they waited for them to begin.

For a moment Alana felt so frightened she didn't think she was going to be able to dance. Then the music began, she looked into Miguel's face and saw the excitement there, and her focus came back. Forget about where you are, she said to herself. Only focus on the dance.

As they danced across the stage, Alana

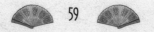

stopped thinking about the audience, or the judges, or the grand theatre. Miguel led her so effortlessly that it felt as though they had been dancing together for years.

When the dance was finished, the audience clapped wildly. Alana and Miguel held hands and bowed, and as they did so Alana glanced at the judges. They looked as unsmiling as ever. Two of them were writing something down, another two were whispering to each other and the fifth one was looking at his watch with a bored expression.

'Well, there's nothing more we can do,' she thought, resigned. 'I've danced my very best, and now we'll just have to hope.'

Chapter 6

Alana and Miguel left the stage, out of
breath and flushed from the excitement of
the performance.

'Come on,' panted Miguel. 'Let's go and
find the others.'

Miguel's family was waiting for them
in the theatre lobby. Everyone hugged
and kissed. 'You were both amazing!'
exclaimed his mother, laughing and
crying at the same time.

Even the baby seemed to know that something special had happened. He clapped his chubby hands and laughed and gurgled.

'But were we good enough?' sighed Miguel. 'That is the question. The other dancers have spent months training for this competition.'

'We can only wait and see,' his mother replied. 'They do not announce the results until this afternoon, so let us go and have lunch.'

'I honestly don't think I could eat a thing,' said Alana. 'I'm too nervous.'

They left the theatre and went to sit in a park nearby.

Miguel's mother had brought a big carrier bag with a picnic.

As soon as she saw the food, Alana realised that in fact she was incredibly hungry. She gobbled her share of the bread and cheese and cold meat, then leant against a tree in the shade and closed her eyes. The family sat around,

discussing the competition and the other contestants.

'I thought the first couple had excellent posture and maintained their close hold throughout,' said Miguel's sister.

'Yeah,' added one of the twins. 'But the second couple kept losing the clipped sharp movements, even though their dance was dynamic and full of drama.'

Listening to their chat, Alana began to realise that this family's passion for the tango ran very deep. It was almost as though their love for the dance was their way of remembering their grandfather. She hoped more than ever that she and Miguel had done OK in the contest.

Before too long it was time to go and find out. They headed back to the theatre, where chairs had been set out on the stage in rows for all of the contestants.

The head judge stood up and gave a seemingly endless speech while the dancers fidgeted in their seats. 'And now,' she said at last, 'I am going to announce the winning couple for the Under 16s.' Everyone on stage held their breath.

'The panel was unanimous in its decision,' the judge continued. 'Many of our couples danced with technical brilliance. However, there was one pair who, while not perhaps as completely polished as some, managed to convey the drama, the passion, the power of the tango more than any other. And it was couple number three ... Miguel and Alana!'

There was an enormous cheer from the

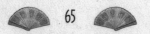

back of the stalls where Miguel's family were sitting, and the rest of the audience clapped politely as Miguel and Alana went forward to shake the judges' hands. Miguel looked overjoyed. He beamed with pride.

When it was over, the contestants filed

off the stage to change. As Alana and
Miguel reached the dressing room, they
found their way blocked by the girl in
the green dress, her faced scarlet with
fury. 'I don't know who you think you
are,' she screeched. 'You have no business
coming out of nowhere and entering this
competition. Taking the prize away from
the proper contestants!'

'Everyone is staring at you,' replied
Alana calmly. 'You may want to speak
more quietly.'

The girl went redder still, but she stood
aside to let Alana and Miguel into the
room.

Then as they were about to enter, a
man tapped Miguel on the shoulder and
led him to one side. 'May I have a word

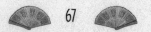

with you?' he asked.

'Erm . . . I guess,' replied Miguel. Alana sat down to wait for him, wondering what the man wanted. Judging from Miguel's face, he hadn't recognised him.

She didn't have to wait long to find out. Miguel came running over looking, if possible, even more excited than when he had heard they had won.

'That was Emilio Escobar!' he declared.

'Great! Who?' queried Alana.

'Emilio Escobar, the famous choreographer!' exclaimed Miguel. 'He says he thinks I have great potential – that I could even become world famous – and he has offered to coach me free of charge. He thinks that I will soon be able to start performing professionally and

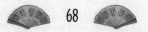

that will mean I can support my entire family!'

'That's amazing, Miguel!' Alana beamed. 'Your grandfather would have been so proud of you!'

'But without you, Alana,' Miguel said, smiling, 'this would not have been possible. After all, it takes two to tango!' He reached into the breast pocket of his grandfather's jacket and drew out the crimson handkerchief. He handed it to Alana. She saw that around the edge were musical notes embroidered in gold thread. 'I want you to have this,' he smiled, 'as a way of saying thank you. My grandfather always carried it when he danced.'

Alana took the handkerchief, but

before she had a chance to say anything in reply, she began to feel the familiar spinning sensation. Madame Coco's voice came to her from far away, saying, 'When your good deed is done, the call of home will beckon. You will return home! You will return home!' The room became blurry and she closed her eyes. She could no longer feel the ground beneath her feet. Madame Coco's voice became louder and louder and the spinning faster and faster until, with a jolt, Alana touched the floor again.

Chapter 7

'Madame Coco,' Alana shouted as soon as she realised she was back in the Costume Emporium. 'I've got it! I know what to do about the Gala!'

'There is no need to talk so loudly, ma petite!' laughed Madame Coco.

'Oh, sorry!' Alana blushed. 'But Madame Coco, do you think *I* can teach the other Step Out Studio students the tango? Do you think I'd be allowed?'

'Well, why don't you ask your Miss Trina,' suggested Madame Coco. 'I'm sure she'd like you to visit her anyway, if she is stuck in hospital.'

'I expect you're right!' replied Alana. And she ran into the dressing room to change. As she passed the grandfather clock in the corner, she was relieved to see that, once again, no time had passed while she'd been away.

Alana was dying to go and see Miss Trina immediately, so she said a quick goodbye to Madame Coco, thanked her once more, and ran home to ask her mum if she was allowed.

'But it's not hospital visiting hours!' said Mum. 'And a good job, too,' she added, 'seeing as you're meant to be looking after Abi right now.'

'It's not fair!' groaned Alana. 'If someone is in hospital, surely you should be allowed to visit them whenever you want!'

'That's not how it works!' replied Mum. 'Visiting times at the hospital are between 2 and 4 p.m. Luckily it's Saturday tomorrow, so you can go then.'

The next afternoon, Alana was at the hospital at 2 p.m. sharp. Miss Trina was sitting in a bed right at the end of a long room. She was reading a book, her leg in a cast and next to her a table covered with flowers and cards, including a big one that the Step Out students had all signed for her. She looked extremely fed up, but as soon as she saw Alana, her expression transformed. Madame Coco was right –

she was obviously happy to be visited.

'How are you?' asked Alana, a bit shyly.
It was weird to see her teacher looking so
helpless.

'I'll be a lot better once they take
this stupid thing off my leg,' Miss Trina
replied ruefully. 'But tell me some news
from the outside world. How are you,

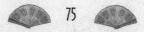

and Meena, and everyone else?'

'Well, actually,' replied Alana, 'I have an idea I want to talk to you about.' And hesitantly, she explained her plan to give tango lessons to the students so that they could perform in the Gala. The most difficult bit was convincing Miss Trina that she would be able to teach the class, when at her last lesson, she hadn't been able to dance the tango any better than the others.

'It's my . . . auntie, you see,' she said. 'She's a tango expert, and she came to stay last week. I asked her to teach me some steps and we spent all of my free time practising.'

She felt bad lying to Miss Trina, but she didn't know what else to do.

Miss Trina looked doubtful. 'You're

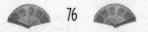

one of my most talented dancers, Alana,'
she said. 'But I really think this may
be too much of a challenge for you. I
appreciate that you want to do this for
Step Out Studio, but the reality is that if
the students aren't properly rehearsed
when they do their show, it'll
mean bad publicity for us.'

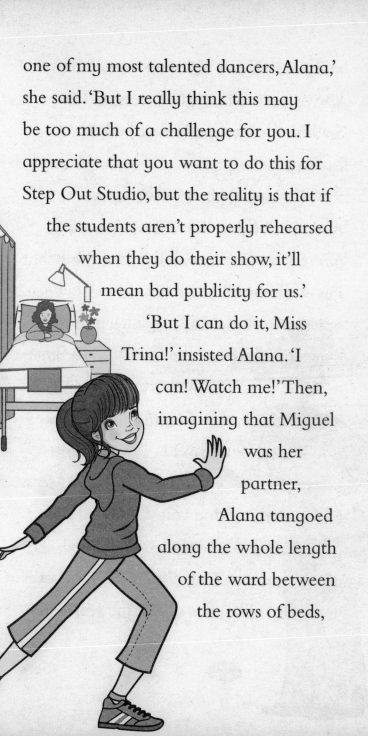

'But I can do it, Miss
Trina!' insisted Alana. 'I
can! Watch me!' Then,
imagining that Miguel
was her
partner,
Alana tangoed
along the whole length
of the ward between
the rows of beds,

being careful not to bump into anything.
The patients all watched in amazement.
Nothing so interesting ever happened in
the hospital!

At that moment, a furious voice
boomed out, 'Just WHAT do you think
you're doing?' Alana skidded to a halt.
The staff nurse had walked out of her
office and was glaring at her,
red in the face with fury.

'I will NOT have
dancing on my ward,' she
bellowed.

'It's my fault, Nurse,' Miss
Trina called. 'I asked Alana
to show me some steps.'

'Well, if she EVER behaves
like that again, she will never

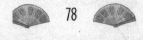

be allowed back here.' And she gave Alana a final glare, then stormed off.

'Thanks, Miss Trina!' whispered Alana, once the nurse was out of earshot. 'She seems seriously scary!'

'She is!' Miss Trina replied. 'Anyway, you've convinced me. I think you can give it a go. Come back tomorrow and we'll plan a routine.'

'Thank you! I won't let you down!' cried Alana. She threw her arms around Miss Trina, then let go, embarrassed. She'd never hugged her dance teacher before.

But Miss Trina looked pleased. 'The days are going to pass a lot more quickly, here, with the Gala to think about,' she smiled.

Chapter 8

The following day was Sunday and
Alana spent the whole of visiting time at
the hospital with Miss Trina, planning the
routine. The teacher no longer seemed
bored and listless – the Gala had given
her a focus, and she looked full of energy.
After Alana's mini performance the day
before, she and Miss Trina had to restrict
themselves to marking out the steps by
hand and writing them down, rather

than actually trying them out. They drew up shapes and patterns with a different coloured pen for each couple.

An old lady in the next bed called Alana over. 'Are we going to see some more of that lovely dancing, dear?' she asked.

Alana grinned. 'I don't dare!' she replied, nodding at the fierce nurse who was keeping a close and watchful eye on her.

After a lot of thinking, she and Miss Trina managed to put together something they thought would work.

'Now the only thing we have to do,' said the teacher, 'is figure out how to get everyone to Step Out Studio to rehearse, without me being there. There has to

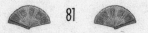

be an adult present at all times – that's the law.'

'Well, how about we ask everyone's parents if they'll take turns supervising?' suggested Alana. 'They can open the studio and lock it at the end, and keep an eye on things. And I'll do the actual teaching.'

'Great idea!' Miss Trina answered, smiling. 'There's a place here where I can use the Internet. I'll ask the nurse to wheel me there – then I can email round the families and set up a rota.'

And so that very week, the students of Step Out Studio filed in to the practice room, with Meena's mum in charge. Alana stood shyly at the front and tried not to panic. 'This might seem scary,' she said to herself, sternly, 'but it's not as bad as competing in the Latin Dance Championships in Buenos Aires, in front of 2,000 people. *That* was scary!'

As soon as the students were ready, Alana told them the plan. She repeated the story about her aunt having given her tango lessons, and explained that she and Miss Trina had thought up a routine together.

'You have got to be joking!' came a mocking voice, when Alana had finished. It was Verity. 'Miss Trina is seriously expecting us to be taught by *you*?'

Alana had been waiting for this. 'It's only for a couple of weeks, Verity,' she replied calmly, 'then Miss Trina should be back in action. And I thought that you could do an introductory speech at the Gala, telling the audience about what a great place Step Out Studio is.'

Verity's expression immediately changed from scornful to smug. She always loved being in the limelight. Phew, thought Alana. The last thing she needed was Verity acting all jealous and trying to undermine her.

'OK,' she said, briskly. 'We need to

begin. Everyone into pairs please. Get into closed hold, and remember your posture.'

Nobody moved except Meena, who obligingly walked to the centre of the room and waited for her partner to join her. The others chatted in little groups, showing no sign of listening.

'Excuse me!' Alana shouted. 'Can everyone please get into position?'

Nothing happened.

Again, Alana forced herself not to panic. She had to be able to control the class, or the whole plan was hopeless.

Without saying another word, she marched off to the props cupboard and took out a gong that had been used for a show the previous Christmas.

Taking the gong back into the studio,

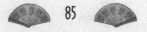

she stood on a chair, and gave it an enormous bash. As the sound reverberated around the room, every student fell silent and stared at her in shock.

'Now,' said Alana, forcing herself to keep her voice steady so that she sounded more in control than she felt, 'do you want Step Out Studio to close down?'

No one spoke.

'Well, DO you?' Alana repeated.

'No,' the students chorused, sounding sheepish.

'Well, if we don't get this dance off the ground, and perform it at the Town Gala, then that's what's going to happen,' she continued. 'So listen to me. I know it's weird having me in charge of the practice sessions, but Miss Trina has explained to me what to do, so really I'm just repeating the things she's told me. Now let's begin.'

Without another word, everyone found their partners, and Alana remembered Miguel's words as she began to teach.

'OK,' she said, 'I want you to promenade into a rock turn, pivot and into an open fan. And remember it has to be precise, elegant and lots of staccato moves.'

'That's good, Toby,' she called. 'Don't forget to keep your knees slightly bent, Keisha.' As the students followed the steps, Alana asked Meena's mum to turn on the music.

By the end of the lesson, the routine was starting to come together. Alana emailed Miss Trina when she got home to report on progress, then the following Saturday she went to visit her to plan what she was going to teach next. Thank goodness Miss Trina will be able to take over soon! she thought.

But when she went to see Miss Trina the following week, she found her looking pale and miserable once more.

'The doctor says my leg isn't healing as quickly as they'd hoped,' she explained gloomily. 'She says I have to stay in hospital.'

So Alana

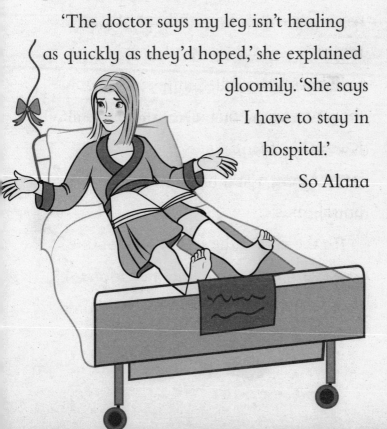

continued to teach, hoping against hope that Miss Trina would be back soon. She never had to use the gong again. She'd proved to everyone that she could lead the class and no one questioned her authority – not even Verity.

By the time it came to the final practice session before the Gala, Miss Trina was still in hospital and Alana was still in charge. When the class was over, she headed home feeling nervous once more. Would the Step Out students pull off their tango routine?

If they don't, it'll be all my fault, she thought.

Chapter 9

On the day of the Gala, Alana tucked Miguel's grandfather's silk handkerchief in her pocket for luck.

Her mum had managed to get the day off work, so she drove Alana and Abi to the Open Air Theatre. When they arrived, the auditorium was already filling up with people.

The Step Out students were the last to come on before the interval. As

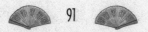

Alana waited for their turn, she stood at the back of the theatre watching the other acts. Among them was Signora Campanella's Ballet School. The girls looked sweet in their matching outfits from Madame Coco's shop. Perhaps some

of them will want to join Step Out Studio when they're a bit older, Alana thought.

When it was the Step Out students' turn to perform, they took their places on the stage, with Alana standing in

the wings to watch. They were wearing costumes borrowed from Miss Trina's props cupboard and they certainly didn't look as striking or as well turned out as Signora Campanella's girls.

Alana peeped out into the audience and her heart leapt. There, right at the front, was Miss Trina in a wheelchair, smiling in anticipation. She must have only just arrived — Alana was sure she hadn't been there earlier. It was obvious that the others had spotted her too. Their faces lit up and Alana could see that having their teacher there had given them a surge of confidence.

Verity stepped forward to do the introduction, making sure to mention Step Out Studio several times during her

speech. Then she took her place next to Matthew and the music started.

Everyone began with a sharp head turn and each couple moved across the floor forming the most dramatic diagonal lines and intricate shapes, just as Alana

and Miss Trina had envisaged when they
mapped it out. Alana felt herself relax
a tiny bit. The tango was definitely the
right dance to choose, she thought. It's so
dramatic and people love watching it. If
any performance is going to make the

 95

kids who are watching want to join Step Out Studio, this is the one.

And it seemed that Alana was right. When the routine finished, the dancers received an enormous round of applause. Some of the audience were even standing. When the clapping died down, there was a buzz of excited chat in the auditorium.

The next thing Alana knew, Miss Trina was wheeling herself on to the stage. She was going to give a speech!

'One of my students has not performed today,' she announced, 'but I owe her a huge amount of thanks. Alana, would you come here, please?'

Blushing like mad, Alana walked on to the stage and stood next to her teacher. Miss Trina told the audience about how

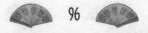

Alana had coached the class while she
was in hospital. Then, after another round
of applause – this time especially for her –
it was the interval.

A group of parents and children
immediately surrounded Miss Trina,

asking her questions. Alana watched them, feeling relieved. 'It looks as though lots more kids are going to want to join Step Out Studio,' she said to Meena. 'And that means everything's going to be OK – Miss Trina won't have to close the school!'

'And it's all thanks to you!' Meena replied.

'Not true!' Alana insisted. 'It's you lot who wowed everyone with your great dancing!'

That evening, Alana took out the gold and purple album she used to record souvenirs of her adventures. She carefully folded up the crimson handkerchief and slipped it inside one of the cardboard pockets. On the outside of the pocket, she drew a picture of a couple dancing the tango, and surrounded them with multi-coloured stars and swirls.

Then she sat cross-legged on the bed, with the album still on her knee, and let

herself dream about the adventure she'd just had.

What will become of Miguel? she wondered. Maybe I will see him perform one day when we are grown-ups. Perhaps he really will become a world-famous tango dancer like his grandfather. And then, who would ever believe me if I told them I'd helped him on his way?

Enter
Arlene's World
of Dance . . .

Become a Tango Star!

Imagine you're dancing in Buenos Aires, just like Alana and Miguel. These special moves will help you perfect a thrilling tango!

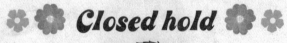

Closed hold

This hold is closer than others in ballroom dancing. Elbows are lifted, and keep your chin up!

Progressive link

A sharp turn. Step back on the right foot, left foot to the side. Turn head and shoulders sharp right.

Reverse Turn

Step back on the right foot, turning
to the left.

Fantastic Tango Facts!

Tango began as an underground dance in Buenos Aires. In the late nineteenth century, tango travelled to Paris where the improvised, spontaneous dance was refined and spread in its ballroom form across the world.

There are several types of tango. The 'Vals' is similar to the Viennese Waltz, danced in 3/4 time, with continual movement and constant turning. Milonga is a version danced in close crowds, so movements are smaller, and music uses a syncopated beat. Argentine Tango is notable for its different hold – the head and chest together, hips apart – which is opposite to ballroom tango's hold with hips together, shoulders apart. All tango styles have no rise and fall and use sharp, elegant, dramatic movements. It is a dance of passion, from the fiery heat of South America.

Out now!
Collect all six
Alana Dancing Star
adventures . . .